PERPETUAL LAW

Mario Bellatin

translated by Stephen Beachy

Deep Vellum Publishing
Dallas, Texas

Deep Vellum Publishing
3000 Commerce St., Dallas, Texas 75226
deepvellum.org · @deepvellum

Deep Vellum is a 501c3 nonprofit literary arts organization
founded in 2013 with the mission to bring
the world into conversation through literature.

Support for this publication has been provided in part by grants from the National Endowment for the Arts, the Texas Commission on the Arts, the City of Dallas Office of Arts and Culture, the Communities Foundation of Texas, and the Addy Foundation.

 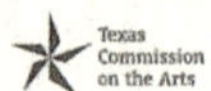   

ISBNs: 978-1-64605-338-4 (paperback) | 978-1-64605-342-1 (ebook)

LIBRARY OF CONGRESS CATALOGING-IN-PUBLICATION DATA

Names: Bellatin, Mario, 1960- author. | Beachy, Stephen, translator.
Title: Perpetual law / Mario Bellatin ; translated by Stephen Beachy.
Other titles: Canon perpetuo. English
Description: First edition. | Dallas, Texas : Deep Vellum Publishing, 2025.
Identifiers: LCCN 2024043126 (print) | LCCN 2024043127 (ebook) | ISBN 9781646053384 (trade paperback) | ISBN 9781646053421 (epub)
Subjects: LCGFT: Novellas.
Classification: LCC PQ7298.12.E4 C3613 2025 (print) | LCC PQ7298.12.E4 (ebook) | DDC 863/.64--dc23/eng/20240923
LC record available at https://lccn.loc.gov/2024043126
LC ebook record available at https://lccn.loc.gov/2024043127

Cover art and design by Lexi Earle

Interior Layout and Typesetting by KGT

Praise for Mario Bellatin

"Mario Bellatin [is one of the] writers without whom there's no understanding of this entelechy that we call new Latin American literature."   —Roberto Bolaño

"Bellatin's extraordinary use of intertextuality and metatextuality draws attention to itself; it is as if his stories were as incomplete as his own body, as his alter egos walking around in his fictional worlds."   —Jeffrey Zuckerman, *Los Angeles Review of Books*

"In a score of novellas written since 1985, [Bellatin] has not only toyed with the expectations of readers and critics but also bent language, plot, and structure to suit his own mysterious purposes, in ways often as unsettling as they are baffling."   —*The New York Times*

"One of Mexico's best-known novelists . . . Bellatin is usually included in a group of post-boom Latin American writers, such as the Chilean Roberto Bolaño and the Argentine César Aira, who have introduced innovations not only in the style of their prose but in the way they think about literature. In Bellatin's stories, the line between reality and fiction is blurry; the author himself frequently appears as a character. His books are fragmentary, their atmospheres bizarre, even disturbing. They are full of mutations, fluid sexual identities, mysterious diseases, deformities."   —*The New Yorker*

"If literature aims to make us less alone, we need writers like Bellatin who reflect not just a different perspective on life, but can envision something separate and apart, a periscope rising above the self."
—Matt Bucher, *Electric Literature*

"Bellatin offers a different way of reading, and of telling, a story—one in which what is unsaid, incompletely rendered, allows respectful room for discovering and conveying more than we might have imagined, or were told that we could."   —Words Without Borders

CONTENTS

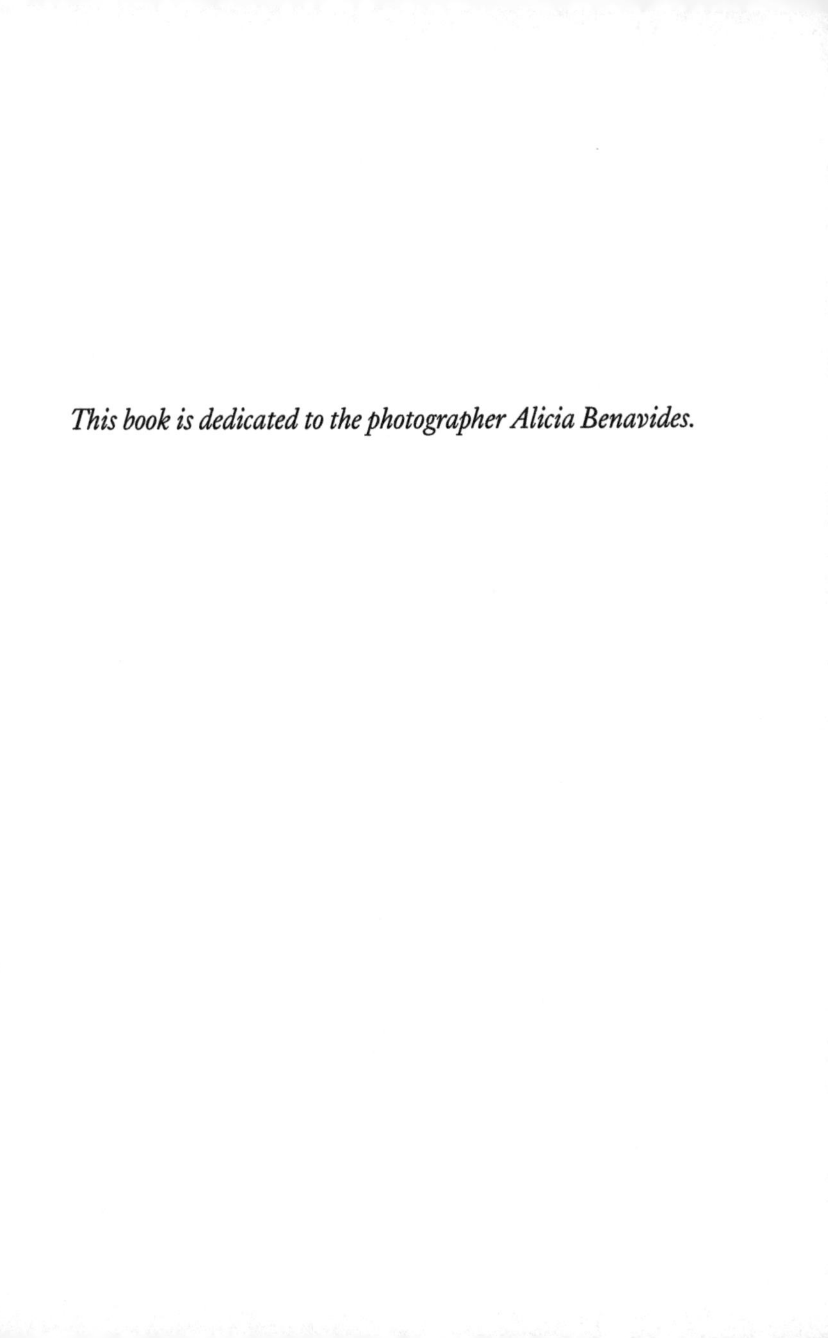

This book is dedicated to the photographer Alicia Benavides.

Our Woman lived in a district where the salty sea air corroded everything. The effects could be seen in electrical appliances, in deck chairs left out on balconies, and in the basic structure of her building. The emergency stairs had been transformed into a heap of twisted iron that the tenants decided to place by the sea, like a grand sculpture.

1.

SOME MONTHS EARLIER, Our Woman had been commissioned to do a feature on the wife of a certain foreign leader who was visiting the country. During a pause in the interview, the foreign leader's wife momentarily left the suite of the hotel where they were just finishing the report. Our Woman couldn't stop herself from stashing a pair of earrings from the head table into her bag. Although the foreign woman's bodyguards noticed the theft, they didn't bother her. The leader's wife returned to the suite, and the interview continued as if nothing had happened. The questions became less engaging, however, as Our Woman distracted herself selecting the most suitable person to give a gift of the earrings she'd just stolen. It was only when she returned to the news agency that her purse was seized by the company's security agents. She tried to offer an explanation. Nobody wanted to hear it. Only her immediate supervisor addressed her, ordering her to await her punishment at home. Our Woman obeyed. She waited a reasonable amount of time but didn't receive any word. Days later, she tried to enter the news agency, but the doorman stopped her. She decided to call instead, and a secretary informed her that she could collect the outstanding portion of her salary from the bank at the end of the month. These events compelled her to spend many hours just lying in bed. She tried to go out as little as possible, but when she did go out, for the rations they distributed every other week, she would tell herself that she really had no right to her share.

One morning the phone rang. To Our Woman, the sound didn't make sense. When she answered, a voice she didn't know began speaking to her. It claimed to be a representative of the House where Our Woman had supposedly put in a request to hear her childhood voice. The petition had been accepted. The voice went on to say that she could come by the House tonight and hear it for herself. A full-length mirror hung in front of the phone. The reflection captured Our Woman's attention and she began studying her own image. She was wearing a synthetic housecoat that concealed a body in decline. She told herself not to be alarmed. It was now time to coexist gracefully with the ongoing deterioration of the flesh. Facing the mirror, Our Woman realized that she hadn't taken a bath in weeks. A slight rash had spread over a sizable portion of her skin. The voice on the telephone was still going on, giving an account of the services the House offered. They had many kinds of voices at the disposal of their clients. Voices of historical figures and of anonymous beings, those of saints and those of assassins. Our Woman was sure that she'd never requested these services, but faced with the insistent voice, she began to believe in the reality of her own petition. She wrote down the address and assured the speaker that she would certainly come. Just saying so brought forth a sensation of powerful heat, a heat that for some reason she hadn't felt in recent days. She became aware of the summer's intensity. She left the apartment and descended the six flights to the basement, stepped over the stagnant puddles on the floor and knocked on the building president's door to ask her to start up the motor for the building's water pump.

The president laughed at her request in a somewhat exaggerated way. Swaying her body, she demanded one good reason to ignite the motor. In forty years, they had never varied the established schedule. Faced with Our Woman's pleas, however, the president seemed to take pity and went back into the caretaker's quarters. After a moment, she came out carrying a full bucket. She would lend it to her, but it would have to be returned just as full. If the bricklayer she'd married came home, it would have to be handed over immediately. Our Woman returned to her apartment and used just half of the water, washing herself meticulously. With her hair still damp, she went out to the balcony to contemplate the sea. She looked at the waves forming in the distance. She looked at the malecón and at the train station located a short distance away. At noon she grew hungry and remembered that in the biweekly distribution she'd been allotted one can of food. She'd saved the can, which contained one hundred grams of beef and was labeled BREAKFAST FOR TOURISTS. She got out a handful of crackers and prepared some sandwiches, then went out on the balcony to eat them. The heat didn't seem to be affecting her. She stretched her body toward the sun and untied her dressing gown.

Her skin was chalky white, with light blue undertones that made it seem even more pallid. In better days, she'd always kept herself tanned. This exaggerated whiteness disturbed her. Annoyed, she got up and went to the kitchen for the remains of the can. There wasn't any meat left, just the liquid it had been packed in. Maybe it was seeing both the sun and the whiteness of her skin that got her thinking she could use the broth to tan her body. She thought she knew something about suntan lotions. During her childhood she'd gotten mixed up with one brand in particular.

When Our Woman was a girl, a competition had been organized in the city to choose a new model for a classic suntan lotion ad. They were searching for a girl who looked like the original model, a girl who was always shown on the beach with a small dog pulling down her bathing suit. Her grandmother was the one who entered her in the competition. Our Woman was sent to a certain address where fifty-eight other contestants were already standing in line. After a somewhat extended wait, some employees came out with a list of names. Thanks to her grandmother, who'd had some dealings with people connected to the firm, Our Woman was one of the girls called. Before showing her in, they took off the eyeglasses she wore to correct her nearsightedness. Once inside, she was told to wait in the corridor. A voice from the room opposite called the girls' names one by one. Each contestant would then cross the threshold and never return. When Our Woman's turn came, she discovered one of the publicists alone behind the door. Although the scene was a blur, the thing that stood out was the publicist's fancy eyeglasses. He was standing to the side of a divan. After he motioned for her to come nearer, Our Woman advanced a few steps and was seized by the arm. She noticed that the lenses of the glasses were green. The publicist got right to work. He reached under her waistband and with a practiced movement lowered her little silk shorts. He paused for a long moment, contemplating the naked ass. He adjusted it in various positions, then just as quickly raised the little shorts, smoothed the child's clothing, and told her to go, signaling a different door than the one she'd come in. Before she left, she was asked what number was hanging from her wrist. Our Woman wasn't chosen. Still, her grandmother convinced her that she was. They got her in the habit of using that particular suntan lotion, and her enthusiasm about going to the beach was usually just a pretext to admire herself in the advertising posters that would begin to show up along the malecón any day.

2.

THE COMPLEX OUR WOMAN lived in had been built by the ocean. Concerned about the onset of August's hurricanes, however, they'd built it at an angle to the sea. From her balcony, she could only partially see the waves coming in. On one occasion, for no apparent reason, the masonry of the dining room's ceiling had collapsed, making a huge racket. The chairs Our Woman had inherited from her grandmother had been unusable ever since. On the ceiling, protruding from the torn-up cement, menacing iron bars were visible. The apartment was nearly full of furniture that recalled the previous epoch. On a little table Our Woman had placed the book *Difficult Loves* by Italo Calvino, loaned to her by the husband of a friend from work. In a section of the living room, she had set up an altar as a kind of tribute to the beings and situations that had most impacted her life. A photo of Marilyn Monroe was displayed on the wall, along with various images of The Beatles from their different eras. Underneath was a portrait of her father seated with her grandmother. To honor her mother, she'd cut out a newspaper article that detailed the heroic act through which she'd lost her life. She also had a photo of Thomas Mann, and another of José Lezama Lima editing a book. At some point, a photo of her little boy had also been posted there, placed between the one of Marilyn Monroe and the one of Thomas Mann. But one morning she'd decided to take it down and replace it with a tiny glass locomotive, along with the cap her little boy had lost before departing. To the side, on a shelf, was the urn with her grandmother's ashes and, hanging from a nylon thread, the various eyeglasses Our Woman had worn while her nearsightedness was getting worse. From left to right, the frames changed in size and varied in style. From the pink ones she wore as a girl, ending in slanted tips, to the square ones she wore before she went through with the operation that corrected her poor vision for good. There was a special compartment in the altar where she temporarily placed objects that she'd stolen, until she could later present them as gifts.

20

From the living room, a pair of doors opened onto the balcony, where Our Woman was accustomed to taking long naps or simply sitting to contemplate the line of the horizon. Now, after smearing her body with the broth from the Breakfast for Tourists, she basked in the sun. She was stretched out on the balcony floor on a towel she'd spread carefully over the warmed-up tiles. Before deciding to anoint herself with the liquid, she'd considered the fact that she had only half a bucket of water left. She would need it for a second bath. As the years had gone by, she'd gained an amazing facility in bathing with a bucket. Since the beginning she had tried to take pleasure in it, imagining herself, when she bathed in this way, in scenes of the Old West that she had seen at the movies. It had been twenty years now since the public baths were shut down. Although it was true that the motor for the water pump maintained a reliable schedule, the water would only ever come out as the tiniest dribble and only from the sink in the kitchen. Not even the sanitary facilities would function with such weak pressure. Our Woman had promised to return the bucket that same night, but it was going to be impossible. She'd have to leave the building earlier than that. The visit to the House demanded it, the House where she'd been promised she could listen to her childhood voice. She'd have to contrive a plan to escape without being seen. She'd have to pay attention to any movements in the basement. Fortunately, the president's routine barely varied.

Without even leaving the caretaker's quarters, the president could maintain control of the tenants all by herself. She relied on two large notebooks she used to note down any suspicious visits or strange behavior she detected. She could only write with great effort, further damaging her weak eyesight every time. With her crushing grip, she would nearly break the pencil that she received each week along with the notebooks. She was obliged to take eggs to the tenants who couldn't attend the official distributions for reasons of work or illness. She also had to wash the clothes of the foreign families, who would buy things from the specialty stores in exchange. Only the sporadic appearance of the bricklayer would change her behavior completely. The husband rarely came around, but when he did, she was obliged to shut herself in with him for several days. The president would only leave her confinement to start up the motor for the water pump. The two of them, the president and the bricklayer, had married for the benefits that came along with a marriage contract. At the Palace of the Newlyweds they'd received some vouchers to buy furniture. They each had the right to a complete change of clothing, and the bride to a veil adorned with flowers of satin, although they had to return the veil afterward. They were also given the opportunity to stay in a hotel for two nights, including use of the cafeteria and the restaurant. It was the bricklayer who came up with the idea of marriage. He had shown up at the building one morning, asking for the president. He'd traveled from the interior, instructed to find her as soon as he arrived in the city. After talking with this stranger, the president put him up provisionally in the antiaircraft shelter under the basement. He was the son of a first cousin. He slept in the shelter for several weeks, until he came up with the idea of marriage and they began maintaining a kind of married life. At first they had worried about the marked difference in age, but they couldn't find a single real obstacle to marriage. They even sent a letter to the first cousin asking her advice and received her blessing by return mail. In no time, the bricklayer had built a cart with metal wheels so that the president could more easily carry the eggs to the tenants and the clean clothes to the foreigners who lived within her jurisdiction.

3.

IN THE MIDDLE of the afternoon somebody banged loudly at the apartment door. Our Woman was still stretched out on the balcony. Eyes closed, she was letting the sun burn her skin imperceptibly. The pounding startled her. The heat was still intense, despite the slight breeze that circulated through the empty window frames. Over the past forty years the actual panes had disappeared bit by bit. The only time a window was broken with actual violence was once when the building was assaulted by one of August's hurricanes. On that occasion, the windows that looked onto the balcony shattered. It was only when the knocking sounded a second time that Our Woman got to her feet. She began tying her dressing gown as she approached to look through the magic eye. It was the bricklayer.

Every time he arrived in the basement, the bricklayer appropriated all of the buckets in the caretaker's quarters. He would also stow away the groceries that belonged to the president and to some inattentive neighbors, so that the two of them could shut themselves up together indefinitely. For days the neighbors would have trouble procuring their eggs and the foreign families would have to find new ways to clean their laundry. The compensation was that they could now freely receive visitors, and some even dared to throw small parties. Our Woman supposed that the bricklayer had noticed the bucket's absence, so she didn't open the door. From where she was standing, the gap in the ceiling was visible. Beams of light penetrated it and fell directly over the parquet floor. During the rainy seasons, she had to cover the floor with a transparent plastic sheet she'd found in the storage room of the news agency where she worked.

The repeated knocking left Our Woman with no alternative but to tiptoe to the balcony. She collected the bucket and the towel and crept into the bedroom. Her skin was bothering her. The liquid from the can had dried, forming a fine film, and she wanted to be free of it. The knocking went on, louder and louder. Our Woman untied her dressing gown and quickly began to wash herself. She didn't care if she splashed the bed or the night table with the water she was scooping up with both hands. She had to hurry, the president had a key to the apartment, and she'd surely end up handing it over to the bricklayer to calm his growing agitation. By the time she'd almost finished the bath, the pounding had turned into violent kicking. It was inconceivable that the neighbors hadn't overheard this scandalous scene. Apparently they were ignoring it. Surely at this hour the majority still hadn't returned from their jobs. Only the children were at home, the sick, the retired, and those who worked graveyard shifts.

After her bath, Our Woman stood naked at the window. She could see the frail body of the president, who was waiting down below. The president wasn't looking up at Our Woman's window, but at the window that looked onto the hallway where the bricklayer could be found, kicking the door. Our Woman ran her hand over her skin to confirm that the liquid from the broth was completely gone. The bucket stood empty at the side of the bed. It was an orange bucket designed to hold two gallons of water. She picked it up, realizing that she couldn't return it now. It was empty, but it could still be very useful for her friend from work. She decided to give it to her as a gift. She would also use the visit to return the book, *Difficult Loves*, that her friend's husband had loaned her, a foreign poet who organized poetry workshops in their house once a week. She returned to the window. Now that her body was clean, she could ignore the bricklayer's pounding. She looked outside but couldn't find a way to get the bucket out through the window. She had considered hurling it to some lower balcony, but the president was still in front of the building. With her arms crossed, she was watching to see what the bricklayer would do next.

Suddenly, Our Woman saw two men come around the corner, walking very close together. They were the same height, and both sported blue overcoats and carried magazines under their arms. At the sight of them, the president hurried into the building. After a few moments, when the men were just arriving at the building's front steps, Our Woman heard her tell the bricklayer to be quiet. She'd climbed the stairs with incredible speed. Her voice was resolute. The silence that followed was total. The men's footsteps could easily be heard on the stairs. Our Woman listened to them climb as far as the third floor. There were only two apartments there: one that was empty, declared uninhabitable, and the other that was occupied by the elderly couple who had once owned the whole building. The men stopped at the door of the old couple's home. Before entering, they would surely post a red paper seal to indicate they were paying a visit. Once again the silence was total. Our Woman supposed that neither the president nor the bricklayer would dare to remain in the open. She was sure that they would shut themselves up in the broom closet at the end of the hall. They wouldn't soon leave. They'd be capable of waiting an hour or more, even all night. They'd only abandon their hiding place when they heard the door on the third floor open again and heard the men's footsteps descending the stairs. Our Woman overcame her fear and began to get dressed. She painted her eyes with a light-colored pencil. She opened the trunk where she kept the gifts she'd received from her father's second wife who, years after the general exodus, had temporarily returned to the country, bearing gifts of clothing and the urn full of Grandmother's ashes. The second wife's other assignment on the trip had been to purchase

a television and a VCR in the specialty shops. Our Woman
fished through the trunk and laid a skirt out on the bed,
one that came to her knees. Also a black silk blouse. She
chose the shoes with the highest heels, and she stretched
a pair of nylons carefully to make sure they didn't have
any holes. She was pleased with her outfit. The only thing
missing was a bag. She didn't have anywhere to carry the
book, *Difficult Loves*, the paper with the House's address,
and the identity card that any police officer on the street
could demand to see. The only bag she owned was the
one they'd confiscated, telling her they'd keep it as proof
of her crime. There was no alternative but to carry her
things in the bucket. After getting dressed and glancing at
the empty space between the photo of Marilyn Monroe
and the photo of Thomas Mann, Our Woman crossed the
threshold without fear.

4.

A PLAQUE WAS DISPLAYED on the wall outside the apartment recognizing the national heroine who had lived there. They'd put it up fifteen years ago. When they'd installed it, there had been a small ceremony in front of the building. They'd spoken at length at that event about Our Woman's mother, who had died by injecting herself with some sort of bacteria while working to create a new vaccine. Our Woman passed in front of the plaque, impulsively pressing her fingers against the metal surface. The plaque would protect her. She was sure that the men in the blue overcoats wouldn't dare to cross the threshold. This thought granted her a certain sense of security, and she went to the end of the hallway and opened the broom closet. Just as she had imagined, the bricklayer and the president were inside. Without giving them time to respond, Our Woman showed them the bucket and shut the door again. As she was making her way toward the stairs, however, she heard the door discretely open. She turned and saw the bricklayer coming out. Our Woman hurried toward the stairs, but he caught her. They struggled in silence. Almost immediately, the president emerged, twisting her mouth into strange grimaces. The only sound was the screaking of Our Woman's heels scraping the floor. Eventually, the bricklayer's strength was too much, and she slipped. She fell gently. It was easy, then, for the bricklayer to take the bucket away. Our Woman tried to hold onto the bricklayer by the legs, but he shook her off brusquely. The bricklayer descended the stairs, stepping as lightly as possible, after first dumping *Difficult Loves*, the paper with the House's address, and the identification card from the bucket. The president had been nervously observing their violent struggle the entire time. She never stopped twisting her mouth into those strange grimaces. She just stood there between the fallen body and the broom closet. As the bricklayer descended, the president tried to follow. Our Woman prevented it. She leapt to her feet and grabbed her by the arms. She was trying to shut her up in the broom closet again. The president resisted, clinging to the memorial plaque. Our Woman pushed her, and the president grabbed her by the neck. She couldn't just leave her in the hallway, but she couldn't get her in the closet either. When it occurred to her that the bricklayer must be in the basement by now, about to enter the caretaker's quarters, Our Woman adopted a more radical attitude. She took the president by the shoulders and began shaking her, letting her head smash against the memorial plaque. Soon, the president's body had gone limp.

The president had had a body that was really quite light. It couldn't have weighed more than a hundred pounds. As Our Woman tried to lift her, she discovered that the back of the neck was wet. Feeling the liquid, she worried that the bricklayer would miss the president and come up to look for her. It occurred to her that if she left the body in front of the apartment on the third floor, even if the bricklayer discovered it, he wouldn't dare do anything about it. Without dirtying herself, she draped the motionless arms over her back and descended the stairs. The president's feet dragged against the steps. One of her shoes, which must have been poorly tied, got left behind, abandoned on the landing. Our Woman didn't run into anybody. When she got to the third floor, she noted that the door did in fact display the red seal. She placed the president on the floor, adjusting her head against the lower part of the door. She arranged it so that the head would fall across the doormat when they opened the door. Our Woman regretted that she didn't have a single drop of water. She would have liked to wash her hands and rinse out some small stains that had soiled her blouse. Trying to find water now, however, would complicate her departure even more. She climbed to the fifth floor to recover the things that the bricklayer had so violently hurled from the bucket. She only picked up the book and the paper with the House's address. She descended again, but instead of heading for the main exit, she continued to the basement. As she'd figured, the bricklayer was shut up in the care-taker's quarters. From inside came a distinct noise, as if he was filling the empty bucket by using a little bit of the water from each of the others. Our Woman left him to his labor. There was no point knocking on the door to con-tinue the fight. It was getting late. Our Woman needed to visit her friend from work and then get to the appoint-ment to listen to her childhood voice. She climbed to the ground floor and went out to the street. When she was

about sixty feet from the building, she began loudly clacking the heels of her shoes. She did it shamelessly. Because
she wanted to walk along the malecón, she had to pass in
front of the emergency stairs that the tenants had decided
to place by the sea.

5.

A SHORT DISTANCE FROM the malecón sat the train station where the train that ran along the coast would stop,
but only very rarely. It was one of the prohibited stations,
and the boxcars would only pass through with their doors
heavily secured. The train passed two times a day. In the
mornings it went toward the north and at night toward the
south. It could run the circuit for an entire year, ignoring
this station completely. But there were times when it gave
a big whistle and then stopped for a few brief moments.
These were the opportunities that some citizens watched
for, hiding in a concrete dugout nearby, waiting indefinitely for the chance to climb aboard the train in secret.
Some broke the windows with their fists, others, armed
with bars, broke down the doors. The concrete shelter,
known as the Dugout of Rapid Departures, was a platform

connected to several underground tunnels. Nobody knew what it had been built for. It was common to see it flooded with water from the city's filtration system. This didn't frighten the citizens who were determined to climb aboard the boxcars. For some reason, despite the repeated violations of the train, their access hadn't been blocked. Our Woman woke up startled every time the whistle sounded, announcing an unexpected stop. She would get to her feet cautiously after reflexively groping for the eyeglasses that she no longer needed. She would go to the balcony, but it was almost always pointless. Before she could see anything, the train would have taken off again. The clandestine travelers generally dressed in black, and painted their bodies too. If they climbed on board at night, they'd have to wait until dawn to feel that the danger had passed. It was said that the first seven hours were the riskiest, as the train could be raided by the authorities in any of the next ten stations.

A few yards before the Dugout of Rapid Departures, Our Woman suddenly left the malecón behind and headed into the city. She went on, clacking the heels of her shoes. She clacked them in front of the police that she passed and in front of the presidents of other buildings.

Just as she'd planned, she made her way toward the home of her friend from work. In one hand she carried the book and, fastened to the elastic of her skirt, the paper with the address of the House. As she passed by a park, she saw more than twenty elderly people doing their exercises. They moved in unison to the commands of their instructor. They were raising and lowering their arms, opening and closing their legs. Their features seemed hardened by the effort. They were lined up in impeccable columns. From a distance, they formed a compact and anonymous group. With the passage of time, the old ones seemed to have lost all individuality, forming a mass in which the small differences in their faces and in their bodies hardly mattered. At some point a familiar noise attracted Our Woman's attention. She heard metal wheels running over the pavement. The president was just receding into the distance at the far edge of the park, pushing her cart full of eggs. Our Woman couldn't believe her eyes. She hurried to catch up, but when she reached the president, she discovered that it was actually somebody else.

She arrived at her friend's home at the exact hour the foreign poet was holding one of his usual gatherings, which he'd christened with the name "Paideia."

The home was spacious and all the members of her friend from work's family had the same right to occupy it. To avoid problems it had been divided into strictly defined sections. Her friend from work had been allotted the foyer and the umbrella closet, along with the living room and part of the kitchen. Her parents made do with the bedroom, the delivery hall, and the other half of the kitchen. Twin sisters owned the dining room, the storeroom, and the balconies. The ex-husbands of the sisters, who had been divorced for some time, lived with their new wives in the garden and in the old servants' quarters. If they had achieved a relative harmony in the division of the space, they hadn't arrived at an accord with respect to the sounds. The mixture of noises from the various televisions, all blaring at high volume, would regularly invade the Paideias that were organized every week by the poet.

6.

As soon as she entered, Our Woman was shown to one corner of the living room. After placing the book on top of a desk, she took a seat to the side of a group of poets from north of the city. A succession of young writers gathered here every week to share and discuss the work they were composing. For his part, the foreign poet introduced his own literary theories. From her spot, Our Woman could easily see the foyer and the umbrella closet. On the central table was a porcelain tureen that contained cold tea. At some point, the doorbell interrupted the foreign poet's discourse. He stopped to answer. Out front were some men, who spoke with him briefly. He returned to the living room and asked to be excused for some business outside. He assured everyone that he wouldn't be gone long. He didn't return for half an hour. He opened the door with discretion and entered in such a way that the young people seated in the living room couldn't see. He was carrying various bags of pants, which he hurriedly unloaded in the umbrella closet. Afterward, he entered the living room and began a polemic concerning the possibility of creating a series of grammatical rules for a new language he was thinking of inventing. Once again, the doorbell interrupted them. The foreign poet stopped, answered the door, and Our Woman could see a young girl hand him a sum of money. He hadn't closed the door before the same men who had rung the first time showed up again. The foreign poet reentered the living room and excused himself again for business outside. In his absence, the young minds of the Paideia fell into a nearly total silence. The poets dedicated themselves to exchanging furtive glances. Without the foreigner to protect them, they must have feared the manifestation of some danger. Her friend from work had met the foreign poet when the news agency sent her to cover a writers' conference abroad. They began a relationship they'd had to interrupt when her friend from work returned to the country. They promised each other they'd meet up again in a few months. Our Woman accompanied her friend from work to the airport after the foreign poet notified her he was coming. Her friend from work wanted the company just then, because she feared she had forgotten her fiancé's face and wouldn't recognize him when he descended from the plane.

In the living room, time was passing, but nothing seemed to happen. Our Woman decided to abandon her seat in the corner. Electric fans had been placed on every one of the little tables, but despite the heat, they hadn't been switched on. A pile of records was spread out on the floor below the bookshelf. Our Woman bent down to examine them and discovered an album by the Beatles. The records were within easy reach, but nobody was paying them any attention. She remembered the many nights she'd stayed up with her boyfriend, trying to tune in to the shortwave frequencies. Back then, there was a special BBC program they liked, but they'd almost always lose the signal in the first few minutes. Our Woman and her boyfriend had to cross back and forth across the whole apartment with the device held up, trying to discover the exact point where they could receive the signal. They'd had to conduct this operation in secret from her mother, who wouldn't tolerate the prohibited broadcasts in her house.

As much as Our Woman wanted to initiate a conversation with her friend from work, the counterpoint between the noise of the televisions blaring from the depths of the house and the total silence of the Paideia made it impossible. She preferred just to leave. Before heading out, she gave her friend a sign. She signaled that she was going and that her friend shouldn't bother to show her to the foyer. As she passed in front of the umbrella closet, she couldn't keep herself from opening the door. Within the diffused brightness, she could make out a transparent bag full of dozens of pairs of sunglasses. Several tape recorders were situated on the floor. On the top shelves were boxes full of Coca-Cola in cans, along with dozens of little hair clips with artificial flowers. Our Woman took a handful of clips. She closed them in her hand, but then put them back just as she'd found them. She turned around to make sure that nobody had seen her and closed the door.

Out on the street it had already begun to grow dark. She checked the paper with the address of the House. She wanted to make sure she remembered the street and the exact address. She realized then that she'd need to retrace her footsteps. The House where she would hear her childhood voice was back at the other end of the malecón. She would necessarily have to pass by the building where she lived. She wouldn't choose to return so soon, but there was no alternative. As she was about to cross the park where the old people were in the habit of exercising, Our Woman saw the foreign poet, off in the distance, hurrying out of one of the specialty shops.

7.

The old people Our Woman had seen earlier were no longer in the park. In their place, another group was forming around the same instructor. Our Woman continued walking without giving them a thought. When she arrived at the seafront, she felt like walking along the entire length of the malecón. After a long stretch, she stopped in front of the Dugout of Rapid Departures. Certain witnesses had told her that her little boy had been sent off from this spot, one day at noon when the train stopped after a long delay. They even gave her the wool cap her boy had dropped in the midst of the confusion. This was the cap she'd now installed in the living room of her apartment. The train didn't always stop without notice. Sometimes stops were established secretly beforehand. What's more, contacts existed who would sell the information at a high price. It seemed that her husband, who had set out with the boy from this place, had paid for the information with the money he obtained by secretly selling a batch of vaccines that had been synthesized by Our Woman's mother before their creation. This only came to light through investigations after the fact. She had also been told that her little boy was wounded as he boarded the train. Our Woman could clearly remember the afternoon she'd gone to recover her little boy from the Children's Day Nursery after leaving the news agency. She was told that her husband hadn't even brought the child that morning. Bewildered, Our Woman headed back to the apartment. She waited without knowing what attitude to take. That night the members of some unfamiliar but official institution knocked at the door. They carried a search warrant that they didn't actually enforce, out of respect for the commemorative plaque on the wall. Our Woman grasped the situation immediately. She threw on some clothes, descended the five floors that separated her from the street, and ran toward the malecón. In less than a minute, she arrived at the staircase of the Dugout of Rapid Departures. She descended the stairs until she arrived at a flooded vault. Her shoes got soaked. The next morning when her friend from work opened her door, she discovered Our Woman taking refuge in the entranceway. Her clothes were wet and she began talking nonstop. Given her physical and mental state, they had to transfer her to a sanatorium, where she remained secluded for more than six months.

From that time Our Woman could only remember the voices that persecuted her at all hours. Dozens of voices surrounded her constantly. There were deep voices and shrill voices, high-pitched voices and low-pitched voices. Some she recognized, others were completely anonymous. As her stay in the sanatorium progressed, the voices diminished little by little until they'd ceased talking for good. When they discharged her, the doctors assured her she wouldn't have a problem maintaining the position that she'd held before the crisis. Indeed, she didn't display any great difficulty readjusting to the work routine. What was more complicated was confronting her apartment again. For a while, her friend from work put her up in her home. Our Woman slept in the kitchen. Her friend from work and the foreign poet slept in turn on a big sofa in the living room, the same sofa where the audience usually sat during the Paideias. When she finally left her friend's home, Our Woman took a book along with her that had pictures of Virginia Woolf. She took it from the foreign poet's bookshelf, perhaps because of a doctor who'd cared for her in the mental hospital. Oddly, she often spoke to Our Woman of the essay *A Room of One's Own.*

The first and most important thing that she did upon returning to her apartment was get rid of any objects that might bring back overly intense memories. The president had to be present for that ceremony. She needed to draw up a record of the discarded items so that they could be tracked and located afterward in other sectors of the population. Our Woman then visited a shop where she stole a small crystal locomotive with the smoke of its chimney frozen in tiny arabesques. She had gone to the shop to acquire some records that might somehow help her to create a new spirit in the apartment, but unexpectedly she came across the locomotives, which were also being offered at a special price.

8.

With her gaze fixed on the Dugout of Rapid Departures, Our Woman didn't notice the slow appearance of her favorite stars. In the sky above the malecón, Epsilon, Antares, and the belt of Orion gradually appeared. As a result of her mother's medical investigations, Our Woman had been relocated an infinite number of times to remote regions of the country. While her mother was visiting small villages in search of the perfectly diseased people to use as research subjects for her vaccine, Our Woman was discovering the world of nature she'd been denied living in the city. Sometimes the towns were so poor that they couldn't even offer them accommodations. There was nothing to do but camp in the outskirts. Bedding down in the mountains inside a sleeping bag, Our Woman entertained herself by identifying the stars. She could only sleep in peace once she'd discovered Epsilon, Antares, and the belt of Orion in the same sky. A lucky sign. Probably the sought-after sick people would appear the very next day, the ones fated to demonstrate exactly the theories that her mother so eagerly sought to confirm.

At some point, Our Woman lifted her gaze from the dugout and continued walking beneath a light turning bluer and bluer. To her side the cars zipped past, coming and going. They disappeared into a tunnel under the sea. Their headlights then reappeared on the other side of the bay. A few minutes later, the silhouette of the emergency stairs that had been placed by the sea took shape against the horizon. The area around the building was deserted. At that hour, the tenants had already returned from their worksites, but hadn't yet switched on the electric lights. The only illuminated windows were those on the third floor. Our Woman understood that the men with the blue overcoats still hadn't left. The president was certainly still reclining with her head leaned just so. The tenants from the floor above must have seen her as they were returning from work, but before responding they would have noticed the red seal in the middle of the door.

Our Woman crossed toward the building, quieting the sound she'd been making with her shoes since she'd left. She went directly to the basement. She had difficulty making her way down. Everything was dark. Only a thread of light escaped from under the door of the caretaker's quarters. Our Woman drew closer and put her ear to the door. Nothing. The bricklayer would most likely be sleeping. After a few minutes, however, she heard something move. Then she heard a splashing, the sound of some gargling, and silence again. The floor of the basement was still damp. Puddles always formed around the water pump and could never evaporate completely because of the area's hermetic seal. The standing waters had rotted away the original floor. It had been eaten away to the point the foundation was visible. That's why the floor was markedly uneven and the drainpipes were exposed. Our Woman didn't know what to do. Even if she knocked, the bricklayer would never open up. Waiting for him to emerge by his own initiative would be a project that could require many days. She went up to the ground floor.

Night had fallen completely. She thought that for the first time in decades the motor for the water pump wouldn't be running. She noticed that the neighbors were trying to produce as little noise as possible. Still, she heard the slam of a door. Probably the men with the blue overcoats. Her first impulse was to make a run for it and hide in the antiaircraft shelter. But she stopped herself at the thought of the metal plaque outside the entrance of her home. She waited, sitting on the steps outside the building. Footsteps descended the stairs. They sounded carefree and light. They seemed like they belonged to someone who either knew each one of the steps perfectly or someone bold enough to risk an accident. She only turned when she heard the footsteps behind her. It was one of the girls who lived on the fourth floor. She was carrying an empty jug in her hand. Perhaps her family had sent her to find water. They must have thought that nothing much could happen to her because of her youth. She set the jug down on the floor and made a couple of gestures to indicate that the president was dead. Our Woman got up and took the jug with one hand and the arm of the little girl with the other. They left the building. With complete confidence, the girl allowed herself to be guided. She surrendered her tiny arm, seemingly with total abandon. Their silhouettes were illuminated only by the lamps of the streetlights. In the middle of the street, the light came down from the apartment on the third floor. Our Woman led the girl as far as the emergency stairs. She left the jug on top of a rusty piece of metal, and they both sat on one of the supports. Our Woman entertained herself for a while running her fingers over the girl's delicate neck. Then she stood and walked slowly toward the building. She went down into the basement, and from one side of the water pump, she grabbed the little gas tank that was used to start its motor, then fueled it up and put it into operation. The noise filled the entire basement. Before leaving, Our Woman went to the antiaircraft shelter and took the box of matches it was mandatory to keep there with the emergency lantern. She left the building behind and walked again toward the emergency stairs that had been placed in front of the sea. Her skirt swayed just slightly. In one hand she carried the gas tank and in the other the book of matches. The girl had disappeared. Only the jug remained on top of the rusty piece of metal. She sprinkled the supports of the stairway with the gas and lit a small fire that died out as soon as it had used up the fuel. She decided then to leave along the perimeter of the malecón. She covered some distance, until she reached a bushy tree and moved away from the malecón to enter the city. She took out the paper with the address of the House in order to check the street and the number again. After one more block, the House came into view— the House where she'd been promised she could listen to her childhood voice.

9.

SHE WAS AT THE door of the House well before the time
set for the appointment. She only realized it when she
saw the clock situated in the upper part of the façade. The
House occupied the middle of an entire block, and she was
impressed by the care with which they'd maintained the
large garden that surrounded it. Our Woman recognized
the architecture as Tudor style, and it surprised her that
along with the bell and some bronze door knockers was a
speaker phone with a video camera. Although it was clear
that the neighboring buildings had had a splendorous
past, the House stood out because its walls weren't dis-
colored and its grounds hadn't been subdivided. What's
more, it was using a system of spotlights much more powerful than ordinary lighting. Our Woman would need to
wait in the next block over. She could just make out some

sort of public establishment. Our Woman walked toward it, curious what it might be. As she approached, she could read the sign by the entrance. PIZZERIA, it said. That it had turned out to be such a place annoyed her. She'd already decided to wait inside until the time for her appointment. She knew that in an establishment of this nature she wouldn't be able to wait as long as she needed. She drew nearer still, and under the word PIZZERIA she could read VITA NUOVA.

She could imagine the place inside. The ceiling, with a heavy fan hanging down, and the floor, covered with grease stains from the pizzas that would drip as the customers squeezed them before biting into them. She could also imagine the noise of the silverware as it cut the meals they were calling spaghetti into the tiniest fractions possible. She suspected it was the only place open in the neighborhood. She entered, situating herself behind a bald man eating rapidly in a seat at the bar. The place was completely full. She chose this man even though she already knew it wouldn't matter how fast he ate. The process governing the arrival and departure of her fellow diners had been precisely calculated. Our Woman remembered having read in the paper that the average diner needed at the minimum three minutes and at the maximum six to consume their order. These calculations had been verified repeatedly, and during the summer season the approximations would vary by decimals at most. Our Woman had to wait more than four minutes for the bald man to finish. She checked both sides of the bar to see how many customers were still eating. When the last one finished, somebody gave the order for everyone to get up. Our Woman watched how the bald man left, handing his dirty fork to the woman they'd posted at the door to make sure nobody carried off the silverware. The busboy immediately began to pick up all the plates. The next round of customers was given the order to take their seats. Our Woman didn't comply, but instead made her way toward the back. She kept going until she came across another worker who was dealing with the dirty plates. Looking him right in the eye, she asked for information about the House. At first the man didn't seem to hear her. He began soaking the dishes in a huge tub full of murky water. Our Woman insisted, and for some reason the worker decided to answer. Without interrupting his labor, he said that some people entered and left the House, but only starting at eight in the evening. Often these people came to the pizzeria afterward. Generally, they'd place their orders in diverse languages or with various idiomatic expressions. They didn't cause any problems, the dishwasher added, since there weren't many options on the menu. Actually, most days the workers couldn't do anything but inform them there wouldn't be any food available until further notice. The fact that they placed their orders in various languages made Our Woman immediately think of the foreign poet. His greatest drama, he had confessed one afternoon during one of the Paideias, involved being without a mother tongue. Since birth, for geographic reasons and because of his family's emigration, he'd had diverse languages at his disposal with which to choose the words or the style that best served him for particular needs. It only became a tragedy at the hour of composing poems. Perhaps this was why he was so interested in creating a new language exclusively for poetry.

Shortly after, Our Woman left the premises. First she had to get past the woman who was checking the silverware at the door. She explained that for lack of time and money she hadn't placed an order. She was only allowed to leave after submitting to a strict inspection. Back outside, she discovered that the House had switched all its lights on, increasing the brilliance that surrounded it. A white luminance spilled from the windows and balconies, and in the trees some colored fluorescent lights had been installed. A line of people had formed in front of the door. She covertly examined their faces. She couldn't find the common feature that usually marked people who shared the same line. The only other time Our Woman had ever found such a feature lacking was in the group of neighbors who gathered once a month in back of the supermarket to wait for the arrival of meat for dogs. She kept looking at the faces. She didn't dare ask questions. She wouldn't do anything more than take her place at the end of the line. After five minutes, just as they opened the doors, two more men joined the line. They were both dressed the same. They wore blue overcoats and read the same newspaper from that morning. Our Woman faltered, wanting to escape from her place. The men were standing just behind her. Nobody but Our Woman seemed surprised by their presence. The others' composure gave Our Woman the courage to turn around and look at the men openly. The two of them were the same height, with the same overcoats, and carrying the same newspaper. She'd have liked to continue establishing similarities, but the line began to move.

They all entered a large reception area, where they were greeted by two girls dressed as nurses. One of the girls gathered the women and the other assembled the men. Both of them slim, each with one red-streaked tuft of hair sticking out from her hairdo. Each carried papers fastened to a clipboard in her hands. The whole time they were inspecting the clients, they were ceaselessly jotting things down with black pencils. Everything seemed to be going according to plan. A powerful air conditioner chilled the atmosphere adequately. Our Woman observed the work of these girls closely. Their task seemed to proceed normally until the inspection arrived at the men who resembled each other. The girls quickly backed away, and one of them used a white telephone on the wall. Our Woman couldn't hear the conversation. After a few minutes, two tall women entered the reception area, very much alike, dressed in evening gowns. Without looking at anyone else, the women took the men who resembled each other by the hand and led them back out through the entrance door. Once they'd disappeared, the girls dressed as nurses continued their labor. The group of

women was led to a large room that opened onto a garden planted with lawn grass. Our Woman was about to
ask where they'd taken the men who resembled each
other, but the stiffness she noted in the girls' movements
stopped her short. It troubled her, this self-censorship.
She'd have liked to defend her right to say whatever she
wanted whenever she wanted. She calmed herself down,
realizing that the very reason for her visit could be endan-
gered if she asked any questions.

10.

OUR WOMAN DECIDED TO wait in silence, but then she realized the petitions were supposed to be made in a loud voice. She figured it out when the first client requested the voice of St. Jeronimo speaking with his dog and his lion. The second client was hoping to listen to what her girlfriends would say when she wasn't around. Our Woman trembled as she requested her childhood voice. To her amazement, nobody seemed surprised. She had feared some sort of smile. A mocking gesture. But her request didn't seem to be out of sync with the usual workings of the House. The only thing that was said, in a kind of whisper, was that it was a simple petition. Maybe that was why she was the first to pass into the garden, and the first invited to enter the little wooden hut that had been constructed in the middle. Curiously, once she was inside,

Our Woman couldn't see or hear a thing. After four minutes of silence and darkness, she was taken out not by a girl, but by a boy dressed as a nurse. She was then led into the interior of the House.

Our Woman had to climb a marble staircase. Along the wall, portraits of various historic figures had been posted. She was sorry Marilyn Monroe wasn't there, whose voice she had always tried to imitate. There was, however, an image of Thomas Mann. She knew his face well. In the sanatorium where she was confined, the doctor who looked after her, the same woman who often spoke to her of Virginia Woolf, gave her *The Magic Mountain* to read as a kind of therapy. Finally, Our Woman was deposited in an office that had been set up in the far reaches of the main balcony. She was seated on a chair in the open air. She looked up then and saw that the sky was covered with stars. She recognized Epsilon, Antares, and the belt of Orion. The sky was clean, like those she'd contemplated while lying in the mountains inside her sleeping bag. Nonetheless, the presence of these stars in the same sky didn't calm her this time. She crossed her legs and, without realizing it, ran her hand over the nylon stockings. She needed to be looked after quickly—surely those women from the ground floor would show up any minute. Just then two men dressed as workers came onto the balcony. They carried the grill of a confessional, which they placed on top of a table. What carelessness not to have had the grill prepared in advance, Our Woman thought. Now she had doubts in the diligence of the House. After two minutes, a metallic voice emerged from the holes in the grill. The voice said that in the little hut Our Woman hadn't been able to hear anything due to certain irregularities that had been discovered in her petition as presented. Apparently, the petitioner had opted for the bartering modality, and the House had realized only too late that what was offered in exchange was very poor. It seemed Our Woman had committed to deliver the voices of some Mongolian peasants during the rice harvest in the year 1896 and of some Central American boys during a baseball game played on an indeterminate date and on an unspecified field. Listening to the complaints of the metallic voice, Our Woman felt ashamed. In her defense, she said that she knew nothing of these matters and that only this morning she had received a mysterious call and was informed of the acceptance of a supposed petition she had made.

The voice affirmed that everything had been a mis-understanding. It informed her that with the bartering modality, the client would always take a loss. The most she could possibly hope for would not be her childhood voice, but maybe that of her nanny. She might also be able to access the infinity of voices that were advertised in the lesser part of the catalog. Regional voices infested with slang terms, idiomatic expressions, or catchphrases. Her claim might also include those of the parrots who speak, in captivity, only from despair. But never those voices more exalted than those of the famous stutterers. Never her own first words which, in the understanding of the House, consisted of babbling and baby talk with so much personality. Full of atmosphere, rhythmical. Our Woman bowed her head and began to cry. The metallic voice went on talking. It said that since an error had been made by the House, they'd do her a special favor. They proposed an exchange between her adult voice and that of her childhood. Our Woman could leave what she now possessed with the House and take away her voice as a little girl. Going forward, she would have to maintain in her daily life the rhythm of her earliest babbling. It would give her a sensation of being surprised each time she pronounced the words. The adult voice Our Woman surrendered would immediately be classified within the section reserved for special cases. The exchange would be beneficial to the House, said the voice that emerged from the grill, since for them it was more important to have a pathological voice than a childish one.

Without giving her time to answer, the boy dressed as a nurse pulled Our Woman up from her chair. He led her inside. As they descended the stairway, Our Woman realized that the metallic voice reminded her of the suntan lotion publicist. Maybe the person hidden behind the grill was the man who'd had the eyeglasses with the green lenses. Surely he was the one who'd provided the House the voice she'd had at the time of the audition. As they arrived at the reception area, Our Woman saw that it was completely empty. The lines that just a few minutes before had backed up from the direction of the little hut in the garden had now disappeared. As they crossed the entryway, the boy dressed as a nurse drew close to her ear to tell her that in the coming weeks the House would be including the president's voice in their catalog. Our Woman had no idea in what section it could be classified. Then the boy left her alone. Our Woman's nerves tensed on suddenly hearing the noises of the street. She could make out certain sounds now that she hadn't heard before she went in. Slowly and without direction she began to walk. The House was left behind, along with the pizzeria whose sign read VITA NUOVA.

Mexican writer **Mario Bellatin** has published dozens of novels with major and minor publishing houses throughout Latin America, Europe, and the United States, including *Beauty Salon* and *Mrs. Murakami's Garden* (Deep Vellum). A practicing Sufi, Bellatin has won many international prizes, including, most recently, Cuba's 2015 José María Arguedas Prize. He lives in Mexico City, Mexico.

Stephen Beachy is the author of the novels *Glory Hole*, *boneyard*, *The Whistling Song*, and *Distortion*, the twin novellas *Some Phantom* and *No Time Flat*, and the Amish sci-fi series that begins with *Zeke Yoder vs. the Singularity*.

www.ingramcontent.com/pod-product-compliance
Lightning Source LLC
Jackson TN
JSHW020421020925
90233JS00004B/12